PRAISE FOR KAREN HESSE'S
JUST JUICE

★ "Like her Newbery Award-winning *Out of the Dust*, Hesse once again celebrates a child's ability to extract beauty, pleasure and even signs of hope from her harsh surroundings. Hesse's poignant story of a family faced with seemingly insurmountable hurdles is filled with small triumphs and momentary insights. This brave heroine will pass the torch to readers everywhere; her courage is infectious."
—*Publishers Weekly,* starred review

"The struggling Faulstich family's strength and the atmospheric details of rural life lend the story a timeless, sturdy quality. This poignant story of love and endurance has a lot to say; fittingly, it never shouts."
—*Kirkus Reviews*

"As in her Newbery winner, *Out of the Dust*, Hesse's plain, beautiful words tell of the harsh dailiness of poverty through the eyes of a child."
—*Booklist*

"A quietly affecting portrait of a young girl doing her best to face some big challenges and a loving family doing its best to get along."
—*The Horn Book Magazine*

"This is a look at contemporary American existence many readers won't know about, and they'll appreciate Juice's strength and determination in the face of adversity."
—*BCCB*

"A memorable main character, and enough complexities to provide ample food for thought."
—*School Library Journal*

Other Signature Titles

Bad Girls
Cynthia Voigt

Bad, Badder, Baddest
Cynthia Voigt

Clockwork
Philip Pullman

Faith and the Electric Dogs
Patrick Jennings

Faith and the Rocket Cat
Patrick Jennings

Katarina
Kathryn Winter

The Music of Dolphins
Karen Hesse

Out of the Dust
Karen Hesse

P.S. Longer Letter Later
Ann M. Martin
and Paula Danziger

Riding Freedom
Pam Muñoz Ryan

*Stay True: Short Stories
for Strong Girls*
edited by
Marilyn Singer

Tru Confessions
Janet Tashjian

just Juice

Karen Hesse

pictures by Robert Andrew Parker

SCHOLASTIC
Signature

an imprint of
Scholastic Inc.

New York · Toronto · London · Auckland · Sydney
Mexico City · New Delhi · Hong Kong

For Kate… just Kate.

ACKNOWLEDGMENTS

Thank you to Lois Blackburn, Brenda Bowen, Eileen Christelow, Heather Dietz, Mark Donald, Louise Duda, Lester Dunklee, Paul Evelti, Rachel, Kate, and Randy Hesse, Hotel Pharmacy, Liza Ketchum, Robert and Tink MacLean, Louise McDevitt, Dr. Eric Millman, Barbara Rocray, Dr. Froma Roth, Officer Steve Rowell, Dr. John Straus, Sue Strong, Leslie Todd, Barbara Vinci, and Kathleen White for your invaluable information, assistance, instruction, and counsel.

ISBN 0-590-03383-2

12 11   1 2 3 4/0

Printed in the U.S.A.   40

First Scholastic Trade paperback printing, November 1999
Book design by David Saylor

CONTENTS

brown paper bags

"Where's Juice?" Ma says, spreading grape jelly so thin on the sliced white bread, you can hardly find the purple. "If she doesn't get herself to school this morning, that truant officer'll be here before I can finish breakfast dishes."

"Won't matter when he comes, Ma," Charleen says. "He won't find Juice, and even if he does, he can't make her stay in school. He'd have to tie her to Miss Hamble's desk to do that."

I hide outside on the back porch, watching them

through the window. My fingers rest on the rough wood. Markey, my oldest sister, looks out at me. But she doesn't make one peep about where I mought be found.

Behind me, the rising sun washes the trees in a yellow light. The quiet fills me.

I don't much care for school, and school, well, it cares even less for me. I should be in fourth grade. But my old teacher, Mrs. Deal, she said I didn't try hard enough and now I must stay back. That didn't stop Mrs. Deal from moving up with the rest of my class. They all left me behind with the new teacher, Miss Hamble.

So I don't go to school much. I spend most days with Pa, walking. Since Pa lost his last job, he does a lot of walking. Being with him beats going to school any old how.

Ma puts a sandwich into each of our three bags and folds the bags shut. I like how neat those folds are. It is like unwrapping a gift, opening the bag at lunchtime. Even after I've used the bag all week and it's limber as a dishrag, I still like opening it and taking out that jelly sandwich. And I like that Ma packs me a sandwich every morning, even if I don't end up eating it in school the way she hopes.

"Juice," Ma calls softly, her round face tilted up to the heating grate in the ceiling. She thinks I'm up there, in the tiny room I share with my four sisters. "Come on down, honey."

I jump off the back porch and clap-hat it around the house. Quietly slipping inside the front door, I hush along the hallway and join Ma and my sisters in the kitchen.

Turtle is the youngest, just over two years, with a head full of orange curls. Next comes Lulu. Lulu has black hair and blue eyes like mine. Ma says Lulu is four going on forty, and sometimes I think she's right. My two little sisters sit under the kitchen table. Lulu is pretend-reading our picture book about the boy and his drum to Turtle. She says the book exactly the way I say it when I'm pretend-reading to her.

Charleen, who is eleven and next oldest to Markey, stands beside the kitchen door. "Hey, Juice," Charleen whispers as I slip in.

"Hey," I whisper back.

Lulu catches sight of me and breaks out one of her best grins. I wave to her under the table.

Markey motions for me to smooth my hair.

I work on a snarl over my ear as Ma comes up. "Juice, honey, you're going to school today."

Ma spits on her finger. She wipes at a smudge on my chin. I lift my head and let her wash me all she wants. That finger of hers reminds me of the ginger cat who washes her kittens down in the Land of the Car Bones, where Pa and I take our walks sometimes.

My stomach growls as Ma spit-scrubs my face. "S'cuse me," I say, grinning. I slap my hand over the noise.

"You're hungry," Ma says. "You can't think on a empty stomach, Juice. How can I send you to school without breakfast?"

I can hardly believe Ma'll let me stay home on account of a growly stomach.

But then I see that is not Ma's plan. She starts to reach for a box of saltines up in the cupboard. But she gets one of her dizzy spells and she holds tight to the sink. I think she gets dizzy like that because she is expecting a new baby, but I don't know. Sometimes I worry it's something more.

Ma asks Markey to fetch the cracker box down for her. Inside the box, one waxed paper stack has about eight crackers left. Ma hands them over to me. I take four out and hand the rest back. "You need to eat, too, Ma," I say.

Charleen puts her hat on. Every day, she wears that little hat tipped back on her head. Ma made that hat for Charleen, braided it out of cloth. Ma's real good with her hands. She makes rugs and baskets to sell in the city.

Charleen thinks when she wears that hat she looks like a picture she saw once of a English girl in a garden. Charleen doesn't look like any English girl.

She looks exactly like Pa and Turtle, carrot-topped and freckled as a guinea egg, from her long, skinny feet to her wide forehead.

I am only nine but already I have feet and hands twice as big as Charleen's, bigger even than Markey's. I don't look like Charleen or Markey, or like Turtle, or even much like Ma or Pa. Just me and Lulu look alike.

But that doesn't mean we don't belong. We sure do. We might not belong to anyone else in this whole world. But us Faulstiches, we belong to each other.

CHAPTER TWO

halfway

I follow my sisters outside and down off the porch. Charleen and Markey slow down enough to keep me between them so I don't give them the slip the way I sometimes can. Billy Altinger's rooster fusses at us, and Brewster Compton's hound flings his old, scarred body against the fence. I feed him a piece of my saltine, and he swallows it down, wagging his tail and sniffing for more.

Charleen picks on me. "How come you feed that dog?"

"Dog's got to eat, too," I say.

"You really coming to school today?" Markey asks, placing her hand on the top of my head as we go.

"I mought," I say.

But I am thinking about school and how hard it is for me. I am thinking about Pa and how lonesome he can get. We pass some blue jays busy on the ground. I toss them a crumb of cracker, and they go beak-pecking crazy, fighting over that teensy piece.

I slow down. Stop walking. "You know," I say. "Pa seemed awful low last night. I don't think I will go to school today."

My sisters nod. They understand me staying with Pa. Pa gets so sad sometimes, makes you feel like you're falling down a hole.

We all look out for him. But I look out for him best, even Ma says so.

"Maybe if Pa had a job . . . ," Charleen says. And we all nod.

Pa has trouble keeping work. Poor as Job's turkey,

that's what the church ladies say we are. Pa's moved us around. Kentucky. West Virginia. Pennsylvania. Mining, mostly, but he takes other jobs, too. He just keeps getting laid off from them. Finally we lit here, in Redemption.

We came here two years ago, because of Grampa Faulstich, Pa's daddy. This house belonged to Grampa's third wife, Miss Jeanette. She died before we ever moved in. When Grampa Faulstich passed over, he left the place to us.

Folks treat us like strangers here. We get visits from the school people and Officer Rusk, the truant officer, and the lady who sells Ma's rugs and hats and pine needle baskets in the city. But no one ever comes to call just to be neighborly. We have chickens like most folks, and a little garden. But with Pa not working at all, life is rough as a cob.

Charleen squints into the branches of a yellow pine. A squirrel flicks down the trunk, chirping as it comes.

Markey puts that worried face on. "Juice, I think

you ought to go to school. You'll never catch up if you don't ever go."

"It's okay, Markey," I say. Gently I pat the back of her hand with my fingertips. "You and Charleen go on. Don't worry." The sun is climbing through the branches of the trees. "Y'all be late if you don't get moving," I say. "I'm heading back now. So I can be there when Pa comes out."

"Doesn't he ever tell you to go on to school?" Charleen asks, kicking a stone. Her toe is almost out of her shoe, so she kicks from the side.

Markey nods. "Pa knows you're not supposed to be home."

"I just say they're mean to me at school, and he takes my hand and walks me the other way."

"Here," Markey says, holding her lunch bag out to me. "You take my sandwich for Pa. I'm not hungry today."

I look at Markey's skinny hand, holding out her brown paper lunch bag. "You don't think Pa would eat your sandwich, do you? Honest, Markey, even taking a bite of mine makes him sadder than a chained dog."

Ma never makes a sandwich for Pa. He goes all day without eating unless I get him to share with me. I don't think Ma eats much, either, even if she is so big. She ought to eat. She gets so funny sometimes. If we make her eat something right away, she gets better. But Ma can be stubborn.

While I stand in the raggedy road, my sisters start walking to school without me, shoulder to shoulder, closing up the little space where I had been in the middle. Half of me wishes I was going down that raggedy road with them. The other half is purely joyful I am not.

CHAPTER THREE

the letter

I wait for what seems like close to a hour. I poke around in the shed beside the house, squeezing between the big oily machines, till Pa comes out. He fills the front doorway for a second.

Coming forward, he sits down on the edge of the porch where the steps mought be.

"Morning, Pa," I say, gazing into his face.

Pa looks like he wants to be cross with me. The best I can get from him is a twitch to his lips. Like there's a smile in there somewhere. It's just not willing to be caught on his face, even for a second. "Morning, Juice."

While he sits, his long legs reaching the packed dirt, he slips a envelope out from under his shirt. He tucks the envelope inside his front pocket. "Your ma says I mought gather some pine needles while I'm out today."

I get down on my knees and reach for the basket under the porch.

Turtle waddles up to the front door. Pa's hand moves to the envelope, covering it. Turtle lets go a string of jabber that makes no sense to anyone but Lulu. "Come back where I can see you, Turtle," Ma's voice calls from inside. Lulu races up, waves at me, grabs Turtle's hand, and the two run back inside the house, squealing.

Pa's hand slides from the envelope back to his lap. I turn the basket upside down and thump the bottom a good bit to get it cleared of dirt and dried leaves.

Taking Pa's hand, I pull him off the porch and

start him to moving. Once I get him walking, he talks. And once he's talking, he doesn't seem half so wore out.

Pa tells me stories about when he was a boy. He tells how he learned to make things with metal from Grampa Faulstich. Grampa Faulstich learned the trade from old man Rogers back in Kentucky. "That old man left Grampa the machines when he died," Pa says. "But he didn't leave Grampa the shop they was sitting in."

Pa has told me this story about old man Rogers a dozen times, but I don't mind hearing it again. It's just that fine, hearing Pa's voice.

"Fat lot of good those machines were to Grampa without a place to use them," Pa says. "He moved those big, old machines from here to kingdom come. What for? They're just collecting dust in the shed now. Just taking up space. You know, Juice, your grampa always talked about building a shop of his own. Never did."

I pick up the long loblolly pine needles. Ma

weaves the prettiest baskets out of those spicy wisps of pine. She likes certain shades best, and I have a good eye for finding them. Pa picks up any old, long needles, green, yellow-brown, tan. Ma is grateful for whatever we bring her. She doesn't go out much herself. Leaving the house makes her nervous.

"Should have stuck with machine work," Pa says, rubbing the sap on his fingers. "I made it to journeyman. No job I couldn't handle. But old man Rogers wouldn't have me. Your grampa took his guff, but I wouldn't. Couldn't hold my tongue back then. I'd be a machinist today. Instead, I went down the mines."

"What about now?" I ask, looking up at him. "Couldn't you be a machinist now?"

Pa lifts his cap off his head. He runs his fingers through his hair, then snugs the cap back on again.

"Grampa Faulstich left all those machines for you," I say.

"It's been a lot of years," Pa says. "I don't remember enough, Juice. And where would I work, anyway?"

I know Pa remembers enough. Pa remembers fiddle songs he learned when he was my age. He must remember.

Pa fusses with that envelope in his shirt pocket. The paper looks important against the worn flannel of Pa's shirt. Every now and again, Pa takes the letter out.

"What's that letter say, anyway?" I ask.

"It's important," Pa says. "It came last week. I had to sign my name before they'd leave it with me."

I never heard of having to sign your name to get mail before.

Pa shows me the top corner of the envelope. "See how fancy that is?" Then he opens the letter and shows me the picture of a building printed there above all the words.

"That looks just like the town office building, Pa. I went there with Mrs. Deal's class last year."

Pa nods. I guess he already knew that, about the town office.

"But what's it say?" I ask.

Pa and I look at each other. He sits down in the pine litter with the letter open in front of him. He rubs his big hand over his forehead.

"I don't know," Pa says. "I can't make out the words."

My heart gets busy in my chest, letting me know it is hearing something that makes it nervous. "Can't you read it, Pa?" I say.

"Aww, Juice," Pa says. "What do you think? I just been needing glasses so long, I can't make those little words out anymore."

I consider his answer awhile.

"Well, Ma still sees good," I say, gathering a bundle of needles, which are half in, half out of the sun. "Ma would read it to you."

I watch to see how he answers this time.

"We don't want to trouble your ma with this, Juice. If she finds out I need glasses so much, she'll

feel bad I can't have them. They cost money, you know. We don't want Ma feeling bad about money."

I think about Ma feeling bad already about the truant officer coming after me with his notices, and her spells, and only jelly for the sliced bread. Pa's right not to worry her more.

I wish I could read the letter to Pa. That would fix everything. But I can't. I am plain stupid when it comes to reading. Everybody else gets it. But reading is pure torture for me.

CHAPTER FOUR

bad news

"I'll get Markey out of class. She'll read the letter to us, Pa," I say.

Pa nods, and we head toward Markey's school.

When we get there, I fox-walk up to the one-story building with its tall windows all in a row. I have to climb up on Ma's basket and look inside each classroom till I find the right one. I take care so no teachers catch me looking in. The basket isn't made for standing on and it gives a little under my foot each time I climb on top of it, but I'm not tall enough to see in the windows without it. While Pa waits back aways with the pile of pine needles, I squint in and find Markey. Her room is near the front of the building.

Markey sits halfway across her class. She leans forward in her chair, listening to her teacher, who is writing something up on the chalkboard.

I stare hard at her. Markey, I think, Markey, look over here.

Esther Winston sees me first and waves. I put my finger to my lips and use my other hand to point at Markey. Esther pokes Elizabeth, who pokes another girl, who pokes Markey. Markey nods when I motion for her to come on out.

I tear back with the basket to regather the pine needles and wait beside Pa for Markey.

A few minutes later Markey slips out the big front door, looks around till she finds us, then comes over.

"My teacher thinks I'm in the girls' room," she says.

Pa gives Markey the letter. She squints and reads the words slowly, to herself.

When she's done, she looks up at Pa. Her dark eyes seem darker than ever. The bones over her eyebrows press toward each other like they mean to have a fight.

"Pa, this letter says we haven't paid our tax bill in nearly two years."

Pa nods. "It's been hard paying bills. We still got debts hanging over from Grampa Faulstich dying."

"Pa," Markey says. "We can't go so long without paying our bills."

"Didn't seem that long," Pa says.

"It says this is the third notice, Pa. What happened to the other two?"

Pa looks down at his cracked boots. "Everybody's looking for money we ain't got. I didn't want to worry your ma. She's having a hard enough time. I tucked those letters away. Figured I'd see to them by and by."

"Pa, according to this, the second letter said unless they heard from us, they were going to sell our house to pay off what we owe in taxes."

"They can't do that," I say. "It's our house. They can't sell it to someone else."

"They can according to this," Markey says, holding up the letter.

"We'll just have to pay the taxes, then, Pa," I say. "That'll make it all right, won't it, Markey?"

But Markey shakes her head. "It's too late for that," she says.

"'Course it's not, honey," Pa says. "It's not too late as long as we own the house. Grampa Faulstich gave that house to us. It's ours."

Markey shakes her head sadly. "Not anymore, Pa. It hasn't been ours for more than a month now, not since the first of September. Our house has been sold to pay off what we owe in back taxes. It belongs to somebody else now."

CHAPTER FIVE

a little light comes on

Markey goes back in to school, and Pa and I walk to town. It takes us something like a hour. We have a truck, but Pa doesn't drive it much. It costs money to keep it on the road.

We don't usually go to town on our walks. With so much country to see, what's the good of wandering in a crowded, smelly, old place, where people look at you like you're first cousin to trouble.

We walk past the sawmill and the lumberyard. We walk past the gas station and the convenience store. We walk past houses, lots of houses, and we keep walking until we get right downtown. Then we walk some more till we find the town office building, the one in the picture. I start up the steps, but Pa hesitates at the bottom.

Turning to him, I catch a worried look on his face.

"Maybe you better wait out here for me, Juice," Pa says.

"I want to come with you."

Pa says, "Juice, it's schooltime. You're not supposed to be walking around town this time of day. You don't want me getting in trouble for letting you miss school, do you? It may make things worse with all this tax trouble. I think you better wait out here."

I sit on the steps and watch over my shoulder as Pa slowly climbs toward the building. He has the letter balled up in his fist as he pushes through the heavy front door.

The mountains rise above the town. They sparkle in the October sun, gold and orange and green. It is better being in those mountains than sitting down here looking up at them. But sitting down here looking up at them is kind of pretty, too.

A man comes by walking a big red dog. The dog stops and sniffs my feet and then my hand, and finally he whuffles his nose around inside my ear. I like the whisper of his breath. I laugh, and the dog wags his tail. In my lap sits the basket, and inside the basket, on top of the long, green-smelling pine needles, is my lunch bag with the grape jelly sandwich. Opening up the bag, one fold at a time, I reach in and break off a corner of my sandwich. But before I can offer the dog a bite, the man jerks him away, tugging him along the street. The dog looks back for a second, regretful. "Sorry, dog," I say.

Now that I am holding my jelly sandwich, I realize I'm hungry. I take a bite off the piece I'd meant for the dog.

Pa comes out just as I am swallowing. I try figuring out what happened in there by the look on his face, but I can't.

"What'd they say, Pa?"

"Well, it's still ours," Pa says. "Sort of. The other folks, the ones who bought our house for what we owed in back taxes, they own the house if we don't pay up. If our debt isn't settled by next September, those folks who paid our taxes for us get our house and we're out."

"You mean if we pay back the taxes the house is ours again?"

"Yeah," Pa says. And he looks pleased. "But we've got to pay all we owed before, and all we owe now, and all we'll owe by next September to make everything even. That's the deal."

"Is it a lot of money, Pa?" I ask.

"Well, it's not too bad, Juice," Pa says. "If I had a steady job. It's not too bad."

"Where you gonna get a steady job, Pa," I ask. "You been looking more than a year now."

"I could go back to the mine. Maybe back in Kentucky. I'd have to live away from y'all. But I could send you money and you could pay off the tax bill, and everything would be all right."

We had tried this once before, when I was little. Pa worked and lived away from all the rest of us. Ma said not one morning, not one evening, not one little piece of the day felt right without Pa. I could hardly remember, but I believe Ma. How could anything be right without Pa around?

"No, Pa." I stand up and cross my hands in front of me, frowning. "You're not leaving us."

Pa growls at me. "Don't talk back to your daddy, Justus Faulstich."

I shrug. Pa is a pretty big guy, but I'm not much scared of him. "You're not leaving us." I fix his eyes with my own and don't let go.

Pa chews the inside of his cheek.

"We'll have to find another way, Pa," I say. "You're not leaving us. You hear?"

I can see Pa's eyes understanding. He knows I'm not giving in on this one.

Pa says, "We got nearly a whole entire year to come up with the money. Till the first of September we have."

"That's plenty time," I say. "It's not even winter yet. Next September is forever away." I grin at him and pull him down beside me.

Pa snaps the suspender holding up my pants. Not so it hurts, just so it makes a little snip of a noise.

"You hungry, Pa?"

Pa eyes my lunch bag. "Nah," he says.

"Well, have some, anyway." I break off a piece of sandwich for Pa and another for myself. "We can't think on a empty stomach, Pa. And we got to do some important thinking. We got to think how we can get our house back."

geneva arrives

Someone is knocking on the front door, but we ignore it. No one but salesmen ever come calling round front. And besides, we are in the back, dancing to Pa's fiddle. Pa fiddles whenever Ma asks. Ma says it soothes her nerves and makes that teensy baby inside her settle right on down. Wait till that baby comes out and finds Pa's fiddle isn't supposed to settle anything down. Pa's fiddle swings us. It sends us sashaying across the kitchen floor. But it does not settle us down.

I don't know how long the person knocks around front.

Finally a face appears at the back door. "Mrs. Faulstich?"

Ma makes her way across the kitchen.

"Mrs. Faulstich, my name is Geneva Long. Is this a good time for a visit?"

Geneva Long is a big woman. Nearly as big as Ma.

Ma says, "Come on, come right on in, Geneva."

For a stranger, Geneva sure looks at home in our kitchen.

Ma's hands are moving fast, clearing a place for Geneva at the kitchen table. "You live nearby, Geneva?"

"Not far," Geneva says. "I come past here twice a day on my way to and from work. I tried calling before I came, give y'all some warning. I'm a home health nurse."

"We don't have a phone," I say.

"What's a home help nurse?" Lulu asks.

Geneva smiles at Lulu. It's a real nice smile. "I

visit sick people in their houses so they don't have to always be going out to the doctor," Geneva says.

Ma likes the sound of that.

"Doctor Michaels heard from the school that y'all might like a visit, Mrs. Faulstich," Geneva says. "He's the one asked me to stop by. I hope I'm not intruding."

While Ma considers, Pa slips out the back door. I think about going with him, but this Geneva, there's something about her makes me want to stay. So I crowd with my sisters onto the old kitchen couch. Lulu climbs straight up into my lap.

Geneva undoes her coat and hangs it over a kitchen chair. It is a nice coat with a fuzzy collar. I can see Turtle wants to get her hands and face into it.

Ma puts out a bowl of sugar cubes to welcome Geneva. Ma keeps the sugar cubes special for when somebody needs a pick-me-up on a torn-down day. They're always there on the shelf, behind the crackers, waiting for if someone beats you up or yells at you or calls you stupid or trash or some such. Or when you fall and split your lip or you get sick and there isn't money for medicine. Or when company calls. That's when the sugar comes out.

Ma offers Geneva a seat, then sits down across from her at the kitchen table.

"When are you due?" Geneva asks.

Ma looks at her fingers, her face calculating. "Probably March. I carry long."

Geneva asks, "You seeing a doctor?"

Ma looks at the five of us. "I've got plenty experience. Haven't needed a doctor yet. Always use midwives. You wouldn't happen to be a midwife, would you?"

"No, ma'am," Geneva says, "Just a home help nurse." And she smiles at Lulu. We all smile back.

Geneva rises up out of her seat and comes to the couch. "So who are you all, anyway?"

Markey introduces us. She says, "I'm Markarita. I'm thirteen. This is Charleen. She's eleven. Justus, here, is nine, Louise is four, and this little one is Turtle. She's two." Markey tickles Turtle as she says her name.

"Turtle?" Geneva asks, bending over to get a closer look at our little sister.

"Turease," Ma says. "We just call her Turtle 'cause she crawled everywhere until she was a year and a half. She was slow to walking. She's slow to talking, too. But so was Charleen and she turned out all right."

We all lean against Charleen, and she pushes us off. But she's shy-grinning the whole time.

"You are some fine-looking children," Geneva says, and I can tell she means it.

Geneva goes back to Ma. "How are you fixed for food, Mrs. Faulstich? Milk, juice, cheese?"

Ma studies the table. "Doing okay," she says. Ma never likes saying how it is with us, especially not to strangers.

Geneva puts her hand over Ma's arm. "The government wants to make certain these good children of yours have enough to eat. I've got cheese right out in the car."

Ma looks over at us. We practically drool on

ourselves at the mention of cheese. Ma says, "We mought could use a little of that."

Geneva nods. She excuses herself and comes back with a black bag in one hand and a box in the other. She puts the box down beside the table and opens the black bag.

"How you feeling in general, Mrs. Faulstich? This feel like all the other times?"

Ma says, "You call me Glory."

Geneva nods.

Ma says, "I don't remember the others moving around so much. Sometimes this little thing gets to kicking so. Not even Lulu moved so much, and I thought certain she was a boy, she was so busy in there."

I lean forward. "Tell her about the dizzy spells, Ma."

Ma shrugs. "Sometimes I get the spells."

"Dizzy spells?" Geneva asks.

Ma nods. "And I get a little confused every now and again."

"Did you get like that with any of the others?"

"Not so's I remember."

"Let me just have a listen," Geneva says. "You mind?"

Ma shakes her head no.

Geneva pulls out a divided hose with a little silver doohickey in the center of it. She has pieces to plug the two ends of the hose into each of her ears.

I hop off the sofa and come closer. Lulu is right behind me.

Geneva smiles down at us. "Stethoscope," she explains. "It can hear the little sounds inside your ma. I'm going to listen to the baby with it right now."

Ma nods and settles in her chair.

Geneva puts the stethoscope on Ma's belly. As she listens, Geneva's head bounces and her lips move and she looks for all the world like she is counting music the way Pa does sometimes with the fiddle.

I pull on Geneva's sleeve. "Can I hear?"

Geneva presses the plugs inside my ears and moves the stethoscope over Ma's stomach. Suddenly I hear *whoosh-whoosh*, *whoosh-whoosh*. Real fast.

"Is that the baby?" I ask.

"It sure is," Geneva says. "That's the baby's heart beating."

I want to hear Ma's heart, too. Then Lulu wants to hear. All my sisters line up for a turn.

Meanwhile Ma and Geneva talk their woman talk. They are taking the size of each other, and Ma, at least, I think she likes the size of Geneva just fine.

"I'll come next week," Geneva says. "Get y'all some more food. Glory, I'd like to run a test on you if you don't mind. I'm a little worried about your blood sugar. How big was Turtle when she was born?"

"Average," Ma says. "Slipped right on out. Never one problem."

Geneva nods and smiles. "I'll bet. Still. It won't hurt to check. Better than you having too much sugar and not knowing."

I shake my head. How could anyone have too much sugar?

the land
of the car bones

I know the big metal building will work as soon as I see it. It is just sitting there, waiting for us, down in the Land of the Car Bones, where all the dead cars've come to rest. I have looked at that metal building a hundred times, but suddenly I am seeing it for the first time.

"Pa, what about that?" I say, pointing to the big metal shed.

"Shorty Lewis used to fix the town trucks inside it," Pa says.

"Where's he now?" I ask.

"At the new garage," Pa says.

"Pa." I try to keep hold of my excitement. "Pa, you could fit Grampa's machines inside there. Every one of 'em."

"You mean . . . use this as a shop?" Pa walks around the building. "I don't know, Juice."

I keep right with him. "It would work, Pa."

Pa pulls off his cap and scratches his head. "I'd need to get it back to the house," he says. "I couldn't come down here to work every day."

"Why not?" I ask. I like the idea of coming every day to the Land of the Car Bones. I love it down here. Just last month I watched the ginger cat have five teensy kittens in the backseat of the green Rambler.

Pa says, "For a machine shop you need power, lots of power. None of that down here. And can you imagine trying to move those machines this far? Besides, it wouldn't be right," Pa says. "This is town land. Town wouldn't like my working here."

"Would they mind if you took the building up to our place?"

"I don't know. We can ask. If nobody else wants it, they shouldn't mind."

The metal building, which Pa calls a Quonset hut, is big. About three large men standing atop each other tall, and maybe three times our house long. I go inside and dance on the dirt under the arched roof. I call out to Pa to come join me. My voice echoes back and forth in the big metal cave.

Pa checks all the places where the frame twists and buckles. He checks where each metal section connects to the next section. Pa studies the bolts. He uses his pocketknife on the patches of rust.

"I'd have to take it apart to move it," he says, his hat in his hand. "Moving each section of metal, and getting it all back together again on some sort of base, that'll take a lot of hard work. A lot of supplies from the lumberyard, too. It's a big job, Juice."

I nod. "Not too big, though, is it, Pa? Not as big as losing the house."

"Nah," Pa says. "Not that big, honey."

We hurry back to the house and check out all of Grampa Faulstich's equipment crammed inside the dark shed, the torches and tanks, the awls and brakes, the lathes and grinders.

When Charleen and Markey come home from school, I grab their hands and run with them to the Land of the Car Bones. I show my big sisters Pa's new shop. We play tag inside, whooping it up, our voices echoing back at us. Markey and I share the secret with Charleen, the secret about losing the house. "Pa doesn't want Ma hearing anything about this tax trouble," I tell Charleen. But Charleen already knows that.

The ginger cat who lives in the green Rambler with her five new kittens purrs when she sees me. Markey and Charleen take turns rubbing the sweet, little, round-bellied things against their cheeks and making *ewey* girl-noises over them. No one in this world is as crazy about animals as us Faulstich girls. I've tried bringing cats home from time to time, but Ma says we can't keep 'em.

"Pa will have work again," Markey says, holding a kitten and looking pleased.

"You'll be able to come back to school," Charleen says.

I scrunch up my face. "Do I have to?"

"Once Pa is working. Sure. He won't need you looking out for him if he's working again," Charleen says.

"He might need me in the shop. He might need me fixing things. He might be so busy, he can't do it all hisself."

Markey puts her arm around my shoulder. "Charleen and I could help you with your schoolwork, Juice," she says softly. "If that's what's worrying you. It's not so hard, if you keep trying."

I shrug her off and stomp away, angry. "I do keep trying," I say.

No one believes me. No one believes how hard I try. No matter what I do, it's never enough.

"Ma'd like you back in school," Markey says. "She's worried about Lulu. Lulu says if you're not going to school, she's not going, either."

Charleen looks at me and laughs. The sound goes everywhere in the metal cave. "What's eating you, Juice Faulstich? You've got the funniest look on your face."

"I don't want Lulu to know," I whisper.

"You don't want Lulu to know what?" Charleen says.

"Nothing," I say, angry.

"What is it, Juice?" Markey says, and she is almost as sweet as Ma when she says it.

"I don't want Lulu thinking I'm stupid."

Markey puts her hands on her hips. "First of all, Lulu thinks the sun comes up in the morning because you make it. And second, you are not stupid, Juice Faulstich."

"I'm not stupid at home," I say. "But I am definitely stupid at school."

Charleen says, "How about this? At night, after dinner, we'll have pretend-school at the kitchen table. We'll tell Lulu it's for her, and you play along. Just so you get used to learning again. Okay, Juice?"

I shrug. But maybe, maybe with my sisters' help, maybe school would make more sense to me.

When we get back home, we find Pa discussing the shop with Ma. Pa says, "It'll cost some to get started, what with replacing the bolts and making a frame for the base and all."

But Pa looks so happy, his eyes shining.

Ma sits down at the kitchen table and gazes across at him, listening to all his plans. Turtle sits at Ma's feet, tracing her swollen toes.

I can tell Ma is fighting with herself, wanting to keep the shine in Pa's eyes but afraid of what it'll cost. Finally, the worried half of her wins.

"Gannon," Ma says, "how are we going to find money for bolts and wood and metal?" She looks sorry as a broken promise having said it.

And she should.

I look over to Pa. Oh, Pa.

He gives up that easy. "You're right," he says. "I don't know what I was thinking," and he hangs his head.

But I am not giving up that easy. "Pa, why don't you talk to the people at the lumberyard? Ask if you can borrow those things from them till you have the money to pay them back."

"We don't do things that way, Juice," Ma says. "That's called credit and it can get you in a heap of trouble. What if Pa can't ever pay back his debt? We're beholden to that lumberyard forever."

I couldn't say to Ma what if we lost our whole entire house, wouldn't that be worse? Pa wouldn't have liked me saying that.

"I could talk to them down at the yard, Glory," Pa says. "Maybe they'd even send some work this way, knowing their payback was riding on it."

"Maybe," Ma says, pushing herself to her feet.

CHAPTER EIGHT

dishes

hen I come to school, Miss Hamble, with her short duckling-yellow hair and her high-up voice, says, "I'm so pleased to see you, Juice." And she means it.

I feel embarrassed when she greets me like that, but a little bit pleased, too.

"I can't be here all the time," I say softly, my head down.

"Honey, it's your job to be here all the time," Miss Hamble says. "It's the most important work you can do right now. I understand you've got things worrying you at home, but you've got to come to school. You understand, sweet pea?"

I feel torn right down the middle between home and Miss Hamble.

Miss Hamble gets me all settled in the room. She tries to make me more comfortable. But after recess, we have reading. Each of us has to take a turn, standing up in front of the class, reading out loud from a big book. When it comes near my turn I pretend I have to go to the girls' room. I wiggle in my seat and cross my legs and wiggle some more. I raise my hand to be excused just before I'm supposed to read. But Miss Hamble says, "Juice, honey, wait till your turn is over."

When she says that, my heart goes crazy inside me. I can't take a turn. I try looking at the book. But nothing makes sense to me. I don't even know what page I should be on. I slam the book down and storm across the room, like I am mad at Miss Hamble for not letting me go when I have to.

Someone says, "Juice is gonna wet her pants."

I spin around. "Am not!"

One of the boys says, "She just don't want to read. She's too stupid."

I hear Miss Hamble as I run out the door. She says, "We don't say things like that in this classroom."

By the time I get home, I'm more knotted than a piece from Lulu's string ball. Not even one of Ma's sugar cubes can sweeten the bitter taste of the day.

That afternoon, Charleen brings home books like the first graders use. Lulu sits on my lap at the table for our pretend school. Turtle marches around the kitchen, banging a wooden spoon on the floor. I listen to Charleen and Markey as if they were learning us about the first day of the world. Pa and Ma listen, too.

But Markey stops as soon as I look up, lost.

"Enough school for tonight," Charleen says.

Lulu wants more, but Markey says, "Lulu, if

you eat too much knowledge all at once, you get a stomachache."

And I tell Lulu that is one hundred percent correct, and Lulu believes me.

Markey and Charleen and Ma hustle Lulu and Turtle off to bed.

Pa gets up and drinks some water.

"What'd they say at the lumberyard, Pa?" I ask.

Pa leans back against the sink. "They said that old Quonset hut is going to be near impossible putting back together once we take it apart. But they said I could run a line of credit up to five hundred dollars. That's standard, they said. Five hundred dollars is more than I need."

Ma comes back in on that last bit of news. "How long will it take to pay back five hundred dollars, Gannon?"

Pa grins. "I don't know. But I mean to find out."

Ma's face rumples a little. "A lot longer than it'll take to spend it, I'll wager." And she rests her crossed arms over her belly. "Juice, go on to bed,"

Ma orders. Then she smiles kind of goofy at Pa. "As for you, Gannon Faulstich, you old business tycoon. Give me a hand with these dishes, why don't you."

And grinning, Pa does.

CHAPTER NINE

lulu gets wheels

It is nearly December, and snow has come twice already.

I'm skipping school more often than not. First, I helped Pa take the Quonset hut apart and move the pieces in the truck, one at a time. Then I helped him put all those pieces back together again on our property. Pa sure can work hard. He said I did good, too.

Pa was right about getting the building back together again. Once we got it apart, that old metal didn't want to remember it ever had fit together. But now we've got the hut standing on its base, and the machines moved in, and most of the roof leaks fixed.

I been helping Ma out, too. Mostly looking after Turtle and Lulu while Ma rests. Geneva said the state would pay for help for Ma. But the aides the state sends don't help much when they come. And then they don't come back again. I pretend-read our picture book about the boy and the drum. I tell the made-up words to my little sisters at least once a day. Lulu says the book to Turtle exactly the same way I say it to her. If I ever get one word wrong, Lulu lets me know.

I have to keep out of sight when Officer Rusk comes. Otherwise he drives me back to school. Miss Hamble wants me to take tests, a lot of tests. I can't take any of her tests. Then she'll know. Everyone will know how stupid I truly am. I couldn't stand that.

Down in the Land of the Car Bones last week, I found a broken bicycle. I go there during the day sometimes so Ma and Pa will think I'm in school.

When I start getting really hungry, I head back. I watch and wait for Markey and Charleen, then walk the rest of the way home with them. Ma and Pa know I'm not really in school. They know as soon as Officer Rusk comes by and tells them. He gives them notices and says I have to go to class. But they can't make me go, not if they can't find me.

The bike from the Land of the Car Bones is a two-wheeler but small, too small even for me. I carried it home and showed it to Pa. He banged the twisted metal back into shape and welded together the snapped bar that held the front to the back. Markey, Charleen, and I cleaned the bike up. We patched the tires and put air back inside them. We gave the bike to Lulu just for nothing, just like that. We could have kept it till Christmas, but once we got it all put together, none of us could wait.

You never saw a girl so scabbed up as Lulu the first few days she owned that bike. Every day she'd show off another bruise, or a skinned elbow, or a bloody lip. But now she can ride anywhere without even a wobble. She pedals slow enough to let Turtle chase her. They tie a piece of string from Lulu's string ball to the back end of the bike, and Turtle grabs hold and they fly around the yard. Turtle is like a kite at the end of Lulu's string. They can keep it up for hours. Ma just sits at the window and watches them. Turtle sleeps so hard at night, she snores.

Word got out that we were fixing old bikes at Pa's shop, and some of the kids from school have come by. Pa lets me help him patch the bikes. We've fixed nearly a dozen so far, some from kids in Miss Hamble's class, some from kids in my old class that is the fourth grade now, and some from kids in Charleen's and Markey's classes.

We don't charge anything to fix the bikes.

Ma thought since it was the only kind of business we had so far, maybe we ought to charge a little something. Me and Charleen and Markey thought so, too, on account of the taxes.

But Pa says, "I'm not charging a little child to fix a bike."

And Ma nods, 'cause Pa is just that good.

Pa spends most of his time cleaning Grampa Faulstich's tools, grinding edges, and fixing the leaks in the shop. He's waiting for some real work to come along.

Markey and Charleen don't teach pretend-school anymore because Lulu and Turtle keep falling asleep at the dinner table and have to be carried to bed. So we don't have to pretend.

But my big sisters keep working with me. When I get tired of trying, we huddle together by the barrel stove, and Markey and Charleen take turns reading aloud, running their fingers along the page to show me what words they are reading. But it all goes so fast, and I can't catch up but with the easy words every now and then.

I notice Pa always makes sure he has some reason to be where we are when I get my lessons, and I wonder whether he can read any better than I can. If Pa can't read, maybe there is no hope for me, either. Maybe there is just something wrong with the two of us, and neither of us will ever learn.

We have fixed all the bikes in the county, and Pa has done some work around the house, but mostly he just sits in the shop, waiting. He is looking sadder and sadder by the day. The shop is cold and huge, and Pa just sits there in the middle of all those big machines, twiddling the wings on a clamp. I figure, the way things are going, I'll have to get him walking again soon, or we'll lose him down the pit of his sadness. We'll lose our house down that same pit, too.

Sometimes, in the evening, for a while there, Pa would pick up his fiddle and play, but now he's put the fiddle away again.

I decide to take matters into my own hands. Surely there's work out there, just waiting for Pa to find it. There are certain ladies who live around in the hills. Some of them are widow ladies. Some of them still have husbands, but those old men are as useless as tight shoes.

I can't write well enough to make a sign saying

about the work Pa does, to hang out for folks to see. But we can just out and tell 'em. So our walking begins again.

Geneva says Ma should go walking every day for her health and the health of the baby, especially on account of the diabetes. Geneva was right about that sugar thing. Gestational diabetes, that's what Geneva says Ma has. It's a kind of disease that happens sometimes to pregnant ladies. When Geneva visits, she sits with Ma and tells her how she needs to watch her diet and exercise and keep testing the sugar in her blood. If there's too much sugar, Ma has to get rid of it with a shot of insulin. If there's not enough, she has to get more inside her. Geneva gave Ma a little pen that springs a blade and gives Ma's finger a prick. Then Ma's supposed to put the drop of blood on a little doohickey Geneva calls a strip and stick the strip inside this teensy machine. When she does it right, numbers come up on a little display that tell Ma how her sugar is doing, whether she has too much in her blood or not enough.

So we take walks together. Pa carries Turtle. Lulu rides along on her bike. And Ma and me, we walk holding hands until we get to the corner. Going at Ma's speed, it takes us ten, maybe fifteen minutes. Then Ma holds Turtle's hand and slowly they head back home, with Lulu doing tricks on her bike all around them. Pa and I keep going, looking for work.

We knock on neighbor doors and ask if there isn't anything metal that needs mending.

"I used to do that kind of work myself," Mr. Wrightson says. But he doesn't have anything for Pa but advice, which Pa listens to but I don't.

Mrs. Lubette says, "The blades on my old mower are broke. You think you could fix them?"

Pa has a look at them. "I could fix that mower for you, Mrs. Lubette."

"I ain't got a lot to pay you."

"Won't cost much," Pa says. "It's just a little job."

While Ma fixes supper, Pa sits down at the table and thinks. You can see how hard he's thinking.

"What you doing, Pa?" Lulu asks.

"I'm making a plan for tomorrow. Figure how much I should charge."

He looks busy with all that thinking, keeping all that important stuff up there in his head. It's like he is seeing himself do the whole job from start to finish. But he isn't so busy he doesn't mind my lesson after dinner.

And that night, the fiddle comes out again. But only for one song.

"Got to get to bed early," Pa says. "Got a busy day tomorrow."

the red car

Markey and Charleen steer clear of Pa's shop, but I can't get enough of it.

Every day after Pa finishes a job, we go out looking for something else that needs doing. Since I brought the bike back for Lulu, I haven't even pretended to go to school. I don't like lying to Ma and Pa.

I never get tired of watching Pa shape a piece of metal into something, like the gutter for Mrs. Thompson's house, or repairing things, like the links in Mr. Opal's chain saw. Pa is a good teacher.

He calls me his apprentice and he says if I work for him for a few years, I could make journeyman and get a job somewhere. I learn what all the machines are for. Markey says, "Doesn't all that stuff scare you? You're awful little around those big machines." But it doesn't scare me at all. Pa's careful about what he lets me do. I feel good in Pa's shop. I feel smart.

Pa tells me how to stay out of trouble when you're using machinery. We can't have any wet spots in the shop. When the roof leaks we have to make certain we take care of it before we start anything else. He tells me to be careful when I handle the pieces of sheet metal. The edges cut like razors. But he only has to show me something once. I might be stupid in school, but if I do something in Pa's shop, I remember how to do it again.

I keep an eye out for Officer Rusk. If he catches me home, he takes me to school every time. He's not mean about it or anything. He just takes my hand, gentle-like, and talks soft to me about how I've got to come to school now. He tells me how Miss

Hamble is worried about me and he puts me in his car. Then he drives over to school. But he doesn't just leave me off. He comes inside and sees to it I go to class.

At school, the kids know I don't belong. Sometimes I act up when it looks like Miss Hamble's about to call on me. Sometimes I ask her a question to get her onto something else. Sometimes I do something funny that gets the class laughing.

When Miss Hamble sends me to the board to do a math problem, I just keep writing things and erasing them until my part of the board is a mess. Miss Hamble explains to me again about those special tests she wants me to take. She says they aren't bad. They aren't anything to be afraid of. But I don't want to take them. Miss Hamble will be so disappointed in me if she finds out the truth about my not reading.

Most important is Lulu, though. Lulu can't know. She can't ever know I don't read. Not ever. As far as I'm concerned, it doesn't matter who else has their suspicions about me, as long as Lulu thinks I'm smart.

During our walks looking for work, I keep my eyes open for useful things. Maybe something Pa can fix, maybe something I can turn into a present for Christmas. Pa and I walk instead of taking the truck. It costs for gasoline and oil, and the tires are mostly bald, and sometimes the engine won't turn over, so we leave the truck behind, except when Pa needs it to do a job.

Pa never does a job right away. He likes to think about it awhile. He spends the evening puzzling out how to do the work so that once he gets the truck going and headed to the job the next morning, he does it all perfect.

I am always looking out for string on our walks. Lulu keeps every piece of string she gets and adds it to her string ball. The ball is bigger than Pa's fist. Lulu keeps it under her pillow and takes it out whenever she has something to add to it.

"Hey, Lulu," I say one afternoon in mid-December. "Go get your string ball."

When she comes back, I reach into my pocket and hand Lulu a long piece of string I found along the road. It is dirty, and Ma insists Lulu wash it before she ties it into her ball.

Ma's right. It wouldn't do having a filthy old piece of string tied to a ball that slept in bed with us every night.

Lulu sets the ball in the middle of the table where Turtle can't reach and goes to the sink to wash the new piece.

"Keep the ball away from Turtle," Lulu says. "She'll eat it."

I roll the string ball toward Markey, and she catches it. A line of string unwinds, making a squiggly little shape on the table. Turtle fusses and points at the string ball and says, "Uh, uh, uh."

Lulu comes over, drying the new section of string on her shirt. "Look," she says, pointing at the squiggle, "y'all made a *w*," and then she makes the shape with her mouth and lets out the sound *w* is supposed to make. Just the way Charleen and Markey taught us to do.

"That's good, Lulu," Charleen says.

Markey shoots a glance at me. I feel angry all the sudden. Lulu will be reading before I can, even if she is five years younger.

Turtle tries climbing up Ma's leg. "Uh, uh, uh," she says, trying to reach the ball of string.

Ma says, "Lulu, honey, put that ball away and play with your little sister. I can't think straight with her climbing up me like that."

Ma is counting Pa's earnings and figuring which bills should get paid. Pa isn't giving Ma everything he makes, though she doesn't know it. Some he is saving out to pay for the taxes to buy our house back.

Lulu puts her hands on my face and whispers for me to watch her string ball. Then she takes Turtle's hand. "Come on, Turtle," she says. "Let's ride the bike."

Turtle grins and tromps out after Lulu. "Ba, ba, ba, ba, ba."

As soon as they are out the door, I place my fingertip over the string, the part that makes a *w*. Closing my eyes, I press down on the squiggled shape of the string. I am always mixing up *w*'s and *m*'s. But now, my finger tells my brain a picture of what *w* feels like.

I open my eyes and look at the string again. Then I look for other *w*'s in the kitchen to see if I can find them somewhere else.

Markey watches what I am doing.

And there it is, on the bread wrapper. The first letter, *W*.

Markey says, "Wonder Bread," and smiles. She makes the *w* sound at the beginning really strong.

"Wonder Bread," I repeat, and I have faith in *w* for the first time.

Charleen and Markey take me through the house looking for *w*'s. We find one on a label in Pa's long johns. We find one on the bleach bottle. I touch the letter and imagine the feel of the string under my fingertip and make the sound like a little wind coming through my lips.

I need to tell Pa about *w*. Racing into the shop, I leave Markey and Charleen behind.

"Pa," I say. "I can read *w*."

Pa puts down the awl.

"I can read *w*, Pa. I really can."

I tell him about the string and my finger touching it and my brain knowing what *w* feels like for the first time.

Pa grins as big as a jack-o'-lantern. But there is something else on his face. Something sorrowful.

Learning about *w*, I feel like a traitor. Like I mought be leaving Pa behind.

I don't want Pa to feel bad. I want to make him happy. I want to tell him I won't love him any less if I can read. Pa and me, we've been careful, tiptoeing around this particular secret. But I can't let Pa's half of the secret keep me from doing something about mine.

When I leave the shop I find all my sisters standing by the shed, Charleen holding Turtle in her arms,

Markey holding Lulu's hand. They all stand staring down to the road.

The road, with its bumps and dips, wouldn't help a car to come along at any great speed. But just sitting there, down at the end of the road, not moving at all, is a old, beat-up red station wagon. It has a dent that runs all the way from the front to the back.

"How long's that car been there?" I ask.

Lulu comes over and takes my hand. "It comes all the time. I see it lots."

I turn to Markey. The bones above her eyes come close enough, they touch.

As we stand there, the red car starts rolling, slow, like the lady inside is using her eyes to eat up our yard and our house and everything as she cruises by. Her eyes meet mine, and I know. She's the one. She's the one who paid the tax money and bought our house away from us.

I let go of Lulu and take a step toward the car.

Then I start to run, shaking my fist.

The car speeds up, drives past the house, past the

line of old trees, and vanishes around the corner by the cemetery.

"She's gone," I say, coming back to my sisters.

My sisters all nod.

And we head in for supper.

a gift

It seems these days the sun no sooner comes up than it changes its mind, turns around, and heads back down again. The hills are bare and thin, shivering under cold and snow.

Pa and me are shivering under cold and snow, too, most of the time. No one is coming by with work for Pa. I thought sure, after they knew my pa was in business, they'd be beatin' a path to his shop. I don't know why they aren't. Seems no one but the school and Officer Rusk and the people from the state want much to do with us Faulstiches. Them and that lady in the red car. And *they* all want *too* much to do with us.

Pa sweeps the floor of his shop. I straighten things. We both wear our warmest clothes. Pa doesn't have a winter coat. He wears his long johns and a couple shirts and a sweater with a hole under the arm. He has wool pants with a flannel liner. They make him look like he's got sausages for legs, but they keep him pretty warm.

Pa welded and bolted together a bunch of metal scraps and made us a big old barrel stove and chimney to use out in the shop. But there's just barely enough wood to heat the house. Wish we had wood on our land. But there isn't any. The old trees along the north side, they go with the cemetery. I think we mought use some of that wood from time to time, but Pa says no.

"How are we doing for tax money, Pa?" I ask.

"I haven't got much saved yet," Pa says.

I look up at him. I thought for sure by now we had practically enough to buy the house back.

"Your ma needs the money. I give her the most of what we earn. It makes her mighty happy, Juice."

"What about the bill down the lumberyard?" I ask.

Pa nods. "I know. I know."

"Pa, you haven't paid on that, either?"

Pa sits down on his stool. "Maybe after Christmas folks'll be thinking about something other than holidays. Maybe then they'll start coming up here to get their things fixed."

"What about *our* Christmas?" I ask.

"Guess we'll have it as long as no one minds."

I groan. "Aw, Pa. Who would mind having Christmas?"

Our Christmases have never been much. Not when it comes to gift giving. But that's okay, I guess. I know some folks get a lot more. Sometimes I wish we could have more, too. But how much does a person need, really? And Christmas with Ma and Pa and my sisters, there's nothing like the warm-inside feel of that.

Pa lets Charleen and Markey and me take a hacksaw out across the creek. We get permission from the neighbors to cut down a little old pine tree in their woods and drag it home. We decorate our tree with strings of popcorn that Turtle keeps trying to eat. We make paper chains instead and hang them.

Pa spends hours and hours in the shop.

I spend hours in there, too. But Pa isn't allowed to look at what I'm doing. And he won't let me peek at him neither. Every now and then the weather goes mild, and I hardly feel the cold at all. It's so nice in Pa's shop. Working back to back. The sound of Pa hammering. The sound of me using the brake to bend the metal around the corners on the little boxes I'm making.

On Christmas morning, we have venison sausage that Geneva made from her husband's last deer. Ma has made candy for each of us. She has also tied up three sugar cubes apiece into little cloth bags. I have made one tin box for each member of my family, the smallest for Turtle and the largest for Pa. The boxes are a perfect size to store the pieces of candy Ma has made us. Pa gives each of us a package wrapped in brown paper and tied with string Lulu claims for her string ball. We open our packages to find Pa has made each of us a plate. Every one with a different design etched into it. The metal plates gleam.

Turtle doesn't give any gifts — she's too little — but Markey and Charleen have made things at school for everyone. And Lulu has gone in with them to make my present. They have glued string onto thirty-six big file cards, one for each letter of the alphabet, and one for each number from zero to nine. Each letter and number is small enough to fit under my fingers. Each card has a picture and a word to go with the letter. Lulu has sacrificed all that string. Charleen and Markey have worked for hours making the alphabet and number cards for me. I am scared all that work won't be worth a thing. Maybe I just got lucky with the *w*. But in my heart I have a big thankfulness for my sisters. And a bigger hope inside me that such a gift should make a difference.

The biggest box I made was for Pa. I was thinking maybe he could keep the tax money in there, but he notices my cards fit perfect, right inside his box. "Maybe you should put those cards in here," Pa says. "So Turtle won't eat them."

I study Pa a second. "I could keep them out in the shop," I say. "I spend more time out there, anyway."

Lulu looks disappointed. "I wanted to play with them."

Markey says, "Lulu, that's Juice's present. I'm sure she'll let you play with her cards anytime you ask. But she can keep them anywhere she wants."

Markey is thinking I don't want Lulu seeing me practicing with the cards because then she'll know I can't read. But really, now Pa can have a chance at learning, too.

We make Ma sit with her feet up on a chair. We clean the kitchen on Christmas day, clean it so it sparkles like the ice on the trees. And when we finish the kitchen, we clean the rest of the house. Pa pitches in and helps, too.

Ma, who is having trouble breathing with all the weight and the baby up under her ribs, cries softly to see the house so nice, and all our beautiful plates stacked up.

"It's a good day," she says. And she doesn't mention once about the lumberyard or the other bills. Not once.

And the beat-up red station wagon doesn't come by the whole day, either.

Charleen says it is because the roads are ice. But I think it is our true Christmas gift.

CHAPTER TWELVE

visitor

Some days the sky spills sheets of ice, some days buckets of sun. On the sun days, when Pa doesn't need my help, and Ma and Turtle and Lulu are settled, and my big sisters are off at school, I study the cards Charleen and Markey made for me. I like some letters better than others. A letter like *o*, that letter just seems friendlier somehow. I keep going back to the letters I think I can trust. But even they don't always do like I think they should.

On the ice days, I huddle by the stove with Turtle

and Lulu, looking after them, looking after Ma. Pa goes out to the shop first thing, and I follow him after I've said the boy with the drum book to my sisters at least twice. On the coldest days, I can't stay in the shop for long. My feet burn, and my fingers get stiff. Every once in a while, I come back in to the kitchen and warm up before I dare Pa's cold again.

But Pa stays with it. He is getting a few jobs now. A couple boys from town came. They wanted to make a ramp and wondered if Pa could help. Folks come up to our place with a log turner, or some busted piece of stovepipe. Pa takes any work. He loves that shop with its black tools and its grimy windows and its strong burning-oil smell. I love it, too. But sometimes it's too cold even for Pa and he comes in and warms his hands and picks up his fiddle and plays for us. In the late afternoons, Charleen dances with Turtle, and Lulu dances with me, and Markey dances easy with Ma until Ma can't dance anymore. And we are all a little jealous that

Markey gets Ma as her partner, but Markey had Ma first and Ma had Markey, before any of the rest of us came along.

I am always looking out for Officer Rusk the same as I am always looking for that red car. But Officer Rusk comes late one afternoon in January. It is already after school, and I'm not watching for him anymore. All my sisters are home when his police car pulls up in the driveway. We wait quietly up in our little room. Pa is away, delivering a piece of pipe special made with three bends in it.

Ma calls me downstairs, and I sit at the table with her, opposite Officer Rusk.

I can hear Turtle breathing through the heating grate and I know my sisters are crowded around, looking through the metal holes, down at us. I hear Charleen shushing Lulu before words get out of her mouth. I sit with Ma and Officer Rusk, looking at my feet. I don't say a word.

"Miss Hamble phoned me today," Officer Rusk says. "She says Justus has been missing school again, Mrs. Faulstich."

Ma nods. "She's been helping me and her pa out quite a bit."

"What about the child care from social services for your two little ones?" Officer Rusk asks. "How's that working out?"

Ma shakes her head. "Not so good. Two or three different ladies came. None of 'em lasted." Ma looks sorry, like it's her fault. But it isn't.

"You have three children of school age, Mrs. Faulstich."

Ma knows that.

"They should all three be going to school."

Ma says, "Juice, here, is a smart thing. She's learning stuff all over the place out in her pa's shop."

"Yes, ma'am," Officer Rusk says. "But the town thinks Justus ought to be taking all that smartness to school with her."

My nose itches. I wiggle it, trying to get some comfort. I keep my hands behind my back. They are kind of black from working in Pa's shop, and I don't think Officer Rusk should see them.

Ma looks helpless. She knows I ought to go to

school. She wants me to go to school. She also knows I hate it. "School is just not calling to Juice right now in a way she can listen," Ma says at last. And she shrugs.

"It is, Mrs. Faulstich," Officer Rusk says. "It is calling for Justus to come to school and stay there until she is sixteen years old. Then it will stop calling if Justus wants it that way."

Sixteen. That is three years older even than Markey.

Officer Rusk hands Ma an envelope.

"Ma'am, this is your final notice. I have to do this. If Justus misses one more day of school, you and Mr. Faulstich, you'll get a court date. It's the law, ma'am. There are consequences for parents who don't get their children to school every day. I'm sorry. Your daughter has a right to an education. It's the law I see she gets it."

I have trouble getting my swallow to go down. It makes a noise that my sisters hear upstairs. Lulu giggles. There is a scuffle up there, sounds like a flurry of bird feathers. Then silence. I feel a grin coming even though I can't let it show up on my face. Not now. Ma would be awful cross if she thought I thought all of this was funny. I don't think it's funny. Just my sisters up there, listening to everything, trying to be so quiet. That's funny.

Ma sets out the sugar cubes in a bowl Pa made. It is one of Pa's prettiest bowls. With maybe ten, fifteen cubes in it, all at once.

And don't they look like a king would eat them, sitting so pretty in Pa's bowl. Pa has made some awful nice things for Ma during the times in his shop when he has nothing else to do.

"No, thank you, ma'am," Officer Rusk says to Ma's offering the bowl of sugar.

He looks sad at being here. Real sad. I feel sorry for him.

"I'll come to school," I say.

Officer Rusk looks at me.

"I'll come. Tomorrow. Tell Miss Hamble I'll be there."

He nods.

"And Officer Rusk?" I say.

He looks at me, right at me, like he's truly interested in what I have to say.

"Officer Rusk," I tell him. "Everybody calls me Juice. Just Juice."

grinning in the rain

eneva comes. She used to come once a week, but now she comes every other day since Ma is less than two months from having her baby. Geneva worries Ma doesn't keep good enough track of how much sugar she has in her blood. But Ma does everything Geneva says to do. I watch her every day. Ma doesn't like doing it, but Geneva says if Ma doesn't, it could be bad for the baby. And that's enough reason for Ma to keep on poking holes in herself even if she hates to. Ma is getting pretty slick at the sticking part. I can watch her do it. Big old Pa, he can't.

Ma shows Geneva the pitcher, the bowl, and the funnel Pa has just made for her.

"He's mighty good, Glory," Geneva says and she sounds almost as proud of Pa's work as Ma. "Does he ever take his things to town to sell?"

My ears perk up.

"Aw, he doesn't have time for that," Ma says. "He's got work enough."

Geneva finishes examining Ma and starts packing her black bag. "Would one of you girls mind coming out to the car and giving me a hand with the box?"

Once a week, Geneva delivers a box full of food from the government: cheese, powdered milk, flour, and cereal.

I follow Geneva and stand beside her car, out in the rain.

"Where could Pa sell his things in town?" I ask, watching the road for the red car. It often comes by this time of day.

Geneva has her head in the trunk of her car. She backs out and straightens up. "What, honey?"

"You asked if Pa ever sold his things down in town," I say. "Where would he go to do that?"

"There's a store on Main Street, Mountain Crafts. Your pa's work would do real nice in there, I think."

Pa didn't have to just count on machine shop work. He could sell things the way Ma did. Maybe the next time the lady came down for Ma's baskets and things, she'd take back some of Pa's work to sell, too.

For the first time in a while, I start thinking maybe we *can* pay the tax bill. And the lumberyard bill, too. I think about all the pretty things Pa has made for Ma, and it's like a light coming on in the darkness and I can see, I can really see a way out of this mess.

I don't care if it is raining. I just stand out by Geneva's car and grin.

CHAPTER FOURTEEN

reasons

I don't think the sun has shown its face one day in all of February. The road is mud, so deep in spots it could maybe close over my head if I stepped into it. Only one good thing about all that mud. The beat-up red car hasn't come by in almost a month.

Ma moves slow, so slow I think pretty soon she mought start going backward.

Pa plans to take his truck filled with plates and lanterns and boxes and candlesticks down to town, to the lady in the Mountain Crafts store. I want to go with him but I want to go to school more. I've been coming pretty regular these past few weeks. I took those tests Miss Hamble wanted for me. I had to read all kinds of words. I tried reading a paragraph, too. Then I had to listen while someone read to me. They asked me questions about what I heard. I even got to play some games, with mazes and such.

Now I spend most of the day with Miss Hamble in third grade. But part of the day I go with Miss Hobarth and two boys from fifth and a girl from sixth, and Ross from Mrs. Deal's class. And we all work on our reading together. The cards Markey and Charleen made for me help a little, but I'm still mighty slow when it comes to reading. Miss Hamble doesn't make me read in front of class anymore. She doesn't make me come to the board, either. She has a quiet, secret way of checking out how I'm doing, and I'm not so ashamed.

Miss Hamble has us putting on a play. She read this book to us. It's about these people who live in a place called Shora. That's in Holland. Holland is another country, like America, only someplace else. And there are these children who live there and they're worried about the storks going away. Miss Hamble makes us pretend we are the different people in the book. Now we're putting it all together into a play. I am Lina. That's the best part in the whole book. Charleen and Markey help me a little, but the words are all mine.

"Miss Hamble gave you the biggest part," Charleen says as we walk to school.

I grin. "I know."

"Why'd she do that?" Charleen asks.

I haven't thought about why Miss Hamble gave me the part of Lina, except maybe she thought I could be real good.

"Maybe she thought you'd come to school regular if you had the part of Lina," Charleen says. "That'd be just like a teacher."

All the sudden I feel a big emptiness inside me. A big ugliness too.

Before I know what I'm doing, I strike out and smack Charleen a good one.

Charleen smacks me right back.

Markey puts herself in the middle, between us, and makes us stop.

My chin is doing that thing it does sometimes when I'm gonna cry. "Do you think that's why I got the part, Markey?" I ask.

Markey gives Charleen a look full of prickers. Then she turns to me. "Juice, you auditioned for Miss Hamble, didn't you?"

I nod.

"And you were the best at pretending to be Lina, weren't you?"

I nod again.

"I'm sure Miss Hamble's glad to have you in school every day, honey, but she didn't give you that part just to keep you in school. She gave you that part because she knew you'd be good. And you are good, Juice."

Charleen nods. "You are."

Charleen looks sorry as a tail-tucked dog for starting all this.

But it's too late. I'm feeling all the sudden like I can't face Miss Hamble today, or the kids in my class. I just want to go home.

I say, "You go on ahead. I think I'll walk back to the house, check on Pa. He might have trouble getting the truck through this mud. He needs to get more things selling in that craft store or we'll never get our house back."

"How much has he saved already, Juice, do you know?" Charleen asks.

I shake my head. "Ma spent a lot of the money Pa made before Christmas, paying bills. Pa hasn't had but a few days without jobs since then, but he's giving Ma most of that money, too. I don't think Pa's much good at saving."

The color rises in my cheeks, just thinking ill of Pa. But in October it seemed we had forever. Now it's near the end of February. Spring'll be coming, then summer. Then the first day of September.

I try putting the right face on things. "It's still a long ways off," I say.

"Not long enough if Pa doesn't save something soon, Juice," Charleen says.

"Maybe the lady in town'll sell all the things Pa brings. She did good with the first few things he brought in," I say.

Markey says, "Pa's doing everything he can."

I nod. "I'll just go back and help him through the mud, then."

"You coming to school after?" Markey asks. "Should Charleen tell Miss Hamble you'll be coming?"

"I don't know."

"Juice, Miss Hamble's counting on you."

I know she is. I shrug. My chin's doing that thing again. I don't want my sisters seeing me cry. I turn my back on them and start for home.

stuck in the mud

"a," I call.

He stands, staring at the mud sucking up the bottom half of his tires.

Pa pulls off his cap, scratches his head, and frowns at the mud.

"Pa," I call again.

Pa looks up. "Stuck," he says.

I nod.

"I'm supposed to meet that lady at the store first thing," Pa says.

"You shouldn't be late, Pa."

"I know."

"You got something in the shop to get you out of this mess?"

"Nah," Pa says. "Can't build a road out of metal. No traction."

"Can we dig it out?"

"Nah," Pa says. "Tried already. Soon as you dig out from the mud you're in, here comes more mud filling in the space."

"What if I dig while you drive?"

We try. It isn't any use. You can't go anywhere if just one tire is free. The other three are still stuck. Ma is in no condition to help, and Lulu and Turtle are too small. Maybe if my sisters had come back with me. I should have made them come back with me.

"Pa, what are we going to do? Is the truck going to be stuck here for the rest of our lives?"

Pa crosses his arms over his flannel shirt. "Mought be," he says.

"Can't be, Pa. You've got to get to town." I can feel the tears trying to get up into my eyes again and

I shake my head like a cat with a flea in its ear. If we leave the truck in the mud, we'll never get the stuff to town, we'll never get the money to pay the taxes, and we'll lose our house for good.

"Gannon!"

We both swing around and turn toward the house.

Ma braces herself in the doorway. She is leaning in such a way I can tell something is wrong, something is terrible wrong.

CHAPTER SIXTEEN

a miracle

"The baby's coming!" Ma yells. She slides down in the doorway, slow motion, and I can hear a groaning sound, the same I heard when Ma brought Lulu and Turtle into the world. It doesn't sound human, the sound Ma is making, but I know at the end, there will be Ma and a new baby.

Pa turns white as chalk. "Get on in and help your ma, Juice," he says. "What day is it? When's Geneva supposed to come?"

"She was here yesterday," I say. "She won't be back till tomorrow."

"Tomorrow's too late," Pa says. "I'll go get her now."

Then he remembers the truck, stuck in the mud.

We race up the driveway together, passing over patches of snow edged with dirt. The earth has that wet spring smell to it; it comes up at me with every footfall.

Pa and I help Ma to the sofa in the kitchen. I never would have believed the kitchen could seem so far from the front door in our little house, but finally we get Ma in there and settled.

"What can I do to help, Ma?" I ask.

I manage to tuck a clean plastic tablecloth under Ma's bottom and get some dry towels.

Pa brings in wood and gets the stove cranking. He looks from me in my muddy shoes to Ma, lying helpless on the old green sofa. Pa makes a funny noise in his throat, then rushes back outside, digging and cussing, cussing and digging, trying to get the truck out of the mud.

Ma pants like a weary dog. Sometimes she makes

that groaning sound and sometimes she folds her face up like it is on a trip somewhere far away. Every now and then she strokes my arm and smiles a sorrowful smile up at me before she starts in that groaning again.

Turtle and Lulu watch Ma, and Turtle fusses seeing Ma act so strange. I give her the last of the oranges Geneva left yesterday, and Turtle stays busy awhile with that.

Ma whispers, "Juice."

I come close to her, stroke her face. She squeezes my hand harder than she means to. It hurts. She never would hurt me on purpose, but she is hurting inside herself and doesn't know she's taking me along with her.

"Juice," she whispers. "Get the little ones out of here, honey. Right now."

I don't know what is about to happen, but I can tell Ma means it.

I think as fast as I can. "Lulu," I say. "I bet you forgot how to ride your bike over the winter."

Lulu looks at me. She is weighing whether I really mean it or I am trying to get rid of her.

"Bi, bi," Turtle squeals and runs to the door, beating it with her little fists. "Bi, bi."

"I bet Pa gets clear of that mud before you even remember the first thing about how to ride a bike."

That clinches it. "Come on, Turtle," Lulu says.

They are out of the kitchen.

"Good job, honey," Ma whispers.

Sweat pours off Ma. She is trembling.

In spite of everything going on in our house, I feel a warmth spread across my shoulder. It's the sun. The sun comes out for the first time in a whole month.

I turn my face to it. "Sun's out, Ma," I say.

Ma doesn't answer for a minute. Then she says, "Go pee in the bushes."

I turn in amazement at what I think I just heard. "What, Ma?"

More silence. Then Ma mumbles something I can't make out.

I don't know if this is what should be happening. I try remembering back to when Lulu was born, but I was so little then. I remember Turtle better. Ma never acted like this when she was having Turtle. This looks more like the spells Ma gets from the diabetes than it looks like having a baby.

The sugar monitor and all the other stuff is beside Pa and Ma's bed. I bring it into the kitchen.

"Ma?"

She doesn't answer. Her eyes look far away.

I try to give Ma the stuff so she can take care of herself, but Ma just lays there on the sofa, looking like Pa did the time he and Grampa Faulstich had too much to drink.

I think about what Geneva mought do if she was here. And I don't like it, but I know what has to be done. I hold that springy little pen against Ma's finger and release it, pricking Ma's skin. I put the drop of blood on the strip and push the strip into the machine.

That's when I feel the panic grab hold. Because all

the sudden it's just me and Ma. And Ma doesn't even know where she is. So that leaves just me to read the sugar numbers. And I have to read them right. If I am going to help Ma, I have to read them exactly right. But numbers are hard, harder even than letters. I remember all those times at the chalkboard, erasing, erasing, making a mess of everything.

I blink hard and look at the read-out that says how much sugar Ma has in her blood.

Ma groans. It doesn't even sound like her. I want her to tell me what to do, but she's in no shape to tell me anything.

I blink again. I think the number says 300. That means Ma's sugar is high, crazy high, and she needs insulin to make all that sugar go away.

I look once more at the numbers.

Not 300.

The number is 030.

I put my finger on the lighted panel. Zero. Three. Zero.

Ma's eyes are open, but she's not seeing anything. She is just groaning. If the number is zero three zero, Ma needs sugar, not insulin. She needs sugar, and she needs it fast. She is not going to get any better unless I get her some. If I'm right.

Where's Pa? I'm afraid to leave Ma long enough to run to the door and call for him.

But I look at those numbers again and I can't get them to hold still.

I race to the door. "Pa . . . ," I start to call.

The truck's gone. Pa's gone. Just Lulu on her bike and Turtle chasing her around the yard.

I race back to Ma. "Pa's gone," I say.

I look once more. Zero three zero. I just have to be right.

"How do I bring up your sugar, Ma?" I ask.

Her eyes are staring up at the ceiling. I can tell she isn't hearing me.

My hands are shaking as I push a chair over to the shelves and climb up and dig behind the cracker box and the noodles until I find the sugar cubes.

I spill cubes all over Ma and the sofa, trying to get one inside Ma's mouth. Once I get one in there, I hold Ma's head so she won't choke on it. I hold her head in my arms and I stroke her wet hair back from her cheeks and her forehead. And when that cube is gone I put another in.

It seems like forever. But Ma slowly comes back from a faraway place. And just in time, too.

She sees the blood sugar monitor beside her. She sees the sugar cubes all over the place. And she squeezes my hand hard, bone-cracking hard. Ma whispers, "It's coming, Juice."

"Ma, you okay?" I ask.

She gives a little nod. "But I need you to do one more thing. You do one more thing, Juice?"

I nod.

"I need you to help the baby out."

Ma tells me what to do, step by step.

I kneel on the sofa, between Ma's feet. I have never seen Ma's private parts before. But I think of the ginger cat down at the Land of the Car Bones and I tell myself this is a good thing. It's a baby coming. That's what I tell myself.

The head pushes out. I can't tell it is a head when I first see it, not until it comes all the way out. But then the head turns and the baby's face, all smushed and puffy, fusses softly, and a shoulder comes. And there are my hands, getting full of slippery stuff and suddenly filled with a whole live, squirming, squealing baby.

"Ma, it's a baby," I say.

Ma laughs real gentle. "What'd you expect, Juice?"

"It's got a little rope attached, Ma."

"There are clean shoestrings in the cupboard, Juice. You need two. Put the baby down and get them."

"You still okay, Ma?" I ask.

"Better every minute, honey," Ma says, sucking on another piece of sugar.

I tie the shoestrings a little apart on the rope leading out of the baby and into Ma. I tie those shoestrings tight the way Ma says.

Then Ma tells me to cut the place in the middle, between the two tight strings, and I do. I bring the baby, wrapped in a towel, to where Ma can see.

She puts out her hands and takes over.

Ma unwraps the baby and examines it, top to bottom.

"You've got yourself another sister, Juice," Ma says.

I grin.

"Your pa's gonna be disappointed," she says.

"Not Pa," I say. "He likes having girls."

"You did a good job, Juice," Ma says. And my chin wobbles again and those tears come back up, but I don't feel beat down by them anymore. I feel big as heaven.

I look at Ma. One of her eyes has a little streak of blood in it from working so hard. Her cheeks are red as cherry Life Savers. But she is smiling and breathing like a person again. And the baby has stopped fussing and just stays put there in her towel with her puckered face all puffy and her eyes all

squinched up. She is huffing like she's just come in from a long run.

I kiss my new sister on her wet forehead. I know that taste.

Ma kisses the baby in the same spot and smiles. "Sugar," she says. And I know that baby has herself a name.

the summons

Pa comes in with Geneva a little after I hand Ma the baby. Pa had packed stones under the tires of the truck and climbed out a little at a time until, finally, he eased the wheels onto paved road. Pa says he made it to the Public Health Office in under five minutes. I don't like to think how fast he was driving to do that.

Geneva says she jumped into her own car and followed Pa and the two of them drove bullets back up here.

Geneva examines Sugar top to bottom, inside and

out. Then she takes care of Ma. When Geneva checks Ma's blood, the sugar level is close enough to where it ought to be.

"I was getting ready to come up here," Geneva says. "I had the bag in my hand when Gannon blew in. I just had a feeling this was the day. I'm sorry I missed the delivery, Glory, but Juice here did one fine job."

The next afternoon, Ma is tucked up on the kitchen couch with Sugar by her side and everybody is sticking to home, even if it is a school day.

Ma turns to Pa. "Did you ever get those things to town yesterday, Gannon?"

Pa's face turns white. "I forgot."

Ma laughs. She says, "Go on and run that stuff down to Main Street. I'm sure the lady at Mountain Crafts will understand when you tell her about the baby."

But not long after Pa leaves, he's back again.

"What's the matter, Pa?" I ask.

Pa is shaking his head. "I was getting the truck started when Officer Rusk, he come up behind me. He come over to the truck. 'How's Juice?' he asks. 'She's just fine,' I say. And I am about to tell him how Juice here delivered the baby when he hands me this envelope and drives away. It looks important, Glory. I thought I better bring it in."

I watch as Pa walks over and gives the envelope to Ma.

Ma takes the envelope. She takes it so natural, like she knew it wasn't doing any good staying in Pa's hands. It is so simple their doing that. If they'd only done that with the tax letters.

Ma opens the envelope and she reads a few words and suddenly her hands are shaking. "It's a summons. To appear in court." There's a scared sound in her voice. A big, scared sound. Sugar starts crying beside her, and Ma gathers up the baby and just in the calming of Sugar, Ma gets herself back under control. "This is because of Juice missing school, Gannon. It says here they can fine us as much as a thousand dollars and we have to pay. A thousand dollars. 'Cause Juice didn't go to school."

Pa sinks down into the kitchen chair, his head hanging low. I've never seen him look as sorry as he looks now, never. And I've seen about every kind of sorry expression on Pa's face there ever could be.

"I'm so sorry, Glory," he whispers.

"It's no more your fault than mine," Ma says.

But Pa only hangs his head lower, like the weight on his neck is just too heavy.

"I can't do it," he says. "I can't do it anymore."

"What can't you do?" Ma asks.

My sisters and I squeeze together. Lulu clings to my hand.

Pa looks at Ma. The look on his face is breaking my heart. "Glory, we've lost everything."

Ma says, "What do you mean, Gannon?"

"We've lost the house," Pa says.

Ma gets up slowly, painfully. She hands Sugar to me while Charleen and Markey help her into the chair right next to Pa. "What do you mean,

Gannon? What do you mean we lost the house?" Her voice is quiet and slow. Just like she is talking to Lulu or Turtle.

And just like that, after all these months of secrets, Pa comes clean about the letters and the taxes. He tells Ma how he was trying to buy the house back, but every time he got a little money saved, something else came up. He tells her how we only have till the first of September, and so far he's saved three hundred and twenty-two dollars. "And now the court says we have to pay one thousand."

Pa stares out the window, his eyes swimming. His two big machinist hands are balled into fists. "If I could read," he says, his voice tearing away at itself. "If I could read, this wouldn't have happened."

Pa looks away, ashamed.

It takes a second to sink in, but then it does sink in and Lulu says, "You can't read, Pa?"

Pa shakes his head.

He looks so hammered down lonely, like he has finally fallen through that black hole I've been holding him back from all this time. But I can't let him go down that hole alone. I look at Lulu. Her face is knotted up, and I know I'm about to be tangled in the same snarl with what I have to say next, but I can't let Pa take it all hisself. It's too much.

"I can't read, either, Lulu," I say.

"Yes, you can, too, read," Lulu says. "You read to me every day."

"I've only been pretending to read," I say. "I tell the way I think the words should go. I never read them. I never have."

And Lulu narrows her eyes at me till I feel pinched in by the smallness of them.

I lose control of my chin, then, and no matter how I work my face, it won't do what I want.

Ma stands and comes over to me. "You can, too, read, Juice. Honey, if you couldn't read there'd be only five little girls here and a foolish old man, and no baby, and no Glory Faulstich."

And Ma tells the story of the sugar monitor. I'd forgotten about the sugar monitor.

"That was just luck," I say.

"No, it wasn't," Charleen says. "That was reading."

The next day Ma and Pa leave Markey, Charleen, and me in charge of Lulu and Turtle and they go down into town with the baby to see Doctor Michaels and drop off Pa's work at the Mountain Crafts store. Ma is nervous about going out, but Pa is with her. She holds on to Pa with one arm and on to Sugar with the other.

As soon as they are out of sight, Lulu pushes Turtle, on purpose, and Turtle falls and smacks her head on the kitchen floor. Turtle starts howling. Lulu yells at her to shut on up.

Turtle catches her breath and comes back crying even harder.

Charleen and Markey gather Turtle up and give her a hug and carry her to our little upstairs room. I can hear them making a big deal out of Turtle wearing Charleen's hat. Bringing Turtle back downstairs, Markey and Charleen gush about how sweet Turtle looks, and she does look sweet, with those orange curls poking out from under the hat, and her face grinning, streaked with dried tears.

I take Lulu's hand, but she pulls away from me for the first time ever since she came into this world. She pulls away.

"Come out to Pa's shop with me, Lu," I beg.

But she won't. She squeezes behind the sofa in the kitchen instead and she won't come out for anything.

lulu emerges

Charleen, Turtle, Markey, and me sit on the sofa in the kitchen the next morning watching Sugar while Ma gets dressed. The baby sleeps in a basket by Pa and Ma's bed at night and by the stove during the day.

Ma comes in looking tired but pretty in her dress of pale roses. Yesterday, after she'd rested up from the doctor, Pa gave her all the letters from the tax collector, and she sat down and read every one in the order they had come. When she got to the last letter, she shook her head, crossing her arms over her chest.

Now, gathering the letters, she folds them in half and tucks them into her handbag. "I need y'all to stay home one more time and look after things."

"What you doing, Glory?" Pa says.

"I'm going down there and talk this over with the tax people," Ma says. "And the school people, too."

We are all amazed at how Ma sounds. Like she could go anywhere in the world.

"Gannon, all these years you did everything you could to take care of us. I'm going to do what I can now to take care of you."

Ma hasn't gone out by herself in so long, I can't remember the last time. But Ma tells Pa to get his work done in the shop. "And you girls, you think you can look after things here? You think you can take care of Sugar?" And Ma feeds her one more time before she leaves.

"She should be fine for a couple of hours. I'll be back long before that."

Sugar snuggles inside the basket as Ma covers her.

"I'll be back," Ma says.

Ma gets behind the wheel of the truck and, slowly, she makes her way along the road, finding the best spots, where the mud hardly rises to touch the sidewalls on the tires.

Pa looks at me and Markey and Charleen. We stare at each other, none of us knowing what to say. And finally, Pa sighs.

"Well, that's that," he says, and he looks in on Sugar, reaches behind the sofa where Lulu has spent the night, coming out only to pee and eat a jelly sandwich. Pa shrugs at Charleen, Markey, Turtle, and me before he walks out to the shop.

We sit on the sofa, staring at our own feet for awhile, when Turtle turns to Markey and says, "Bi?"

"Hey, Lulu," Charleen says. "Turtle wants to play bike."

Lulu moves around behind the sofa, but she doesn't say a word.

"Come on, Lulu," Charleen says.

But Lulu ignores us.

"Suit yourself," Charleen says. She and Markey

head outside with Turtle. I stay in with Lulu behind me and Sugar sleeping in the basket by the stove. The whole house has a smell to it, like Ma's neck. If we left, I wonder, would the house still have that smell? Would it if the lady in the red car lived here instead?

In the basket, Sugar cries out. I hurry over, and she wiggles in her little bed. Gently I pat her back. "Sssshhhhh, ssssshhhhhh," I whisper. She squirms for a few minutes more. Then she passes some wind. For a little baby, it makes a lot of noise. Lulu giggles from behind the sofa. I look in at my littlest sister. She has settled down to sleep again with a crooked smile on her face. "She looks pretty pleased with herself," I say.

Lulu pushes on the sofa so it moves a little. She is giving it little kicks with her feet.

"I thought Pa knew everything," she says.

"Well, he does, almost, Lu," I say. "He can make anything from a piece of metal, can't he?"

She doesn't answer.

"Can't he?"

"I guess," she says.

"And he can play fiddle so you can't hold your bones still."

Silence again.

"Lulu?"

Her head appears from behind the sofa. It looks like when Sugar was being born. Just a head with no body attached. Just a head being born out of the sofa.

"Why should I listen to you? You lied to me. You can't even read."

"I can," I say. "A little. And I'm sorry I lied to you, Lu. Truly I am."

Lulu looks at me. "Juice, if we can't stay in our house, where will we live? In Pa's shop? In the Land of the Car Bones? I hate both those places. They scare me."

"I don't know where we'll live, Lu, but don't be scared. Ma and Pa will take care of you. I'll take care of you. I promise."

And I can see, I can see that after everything she still believes me.

Looking out the window, I watch Markey and Charleen on either side of the bike, and in the middle is Turtle. They hold her on the bike seat and drive her around the muddy yard. All three of them are laughing so hard, I can hear them like a song through the window glass.

I don't want to leave this house any more than my sister does. I don't want one thing to change.

"Turtle's riding your bike," I tell Lulu.

"Where?" Lulu struggles out from behind the sofa and rushes over to the window.

Together, we watch as Turtle's legs stick straight out on either side and she crows with joy at the feel of the spring wind in her face. They aren't moving but about as slow as a drip forming, but Turtle looks fine up there, her hair dancing in the breeze.

"Great. Now she'll want to ride it all the time," Lulu says.

Sugar wakes for good, and I change her diaper, a really black, muddy, sticky, yucky, disgusting diaper. Lulu makes gagging noises, but I get her to help, anyway.

When we finally get the baby washed up, Lulu makes faces and talks to Sugar while I get myself cleaned up, too.

Ma is not back yet. I have to remind myself she hasn't been gone all that long. It just seems that way.

Markey and Charleen come in with Turtle.

Wrapping Sugar up tight in a blanket, Markey carries her outside to get her some sunshine and fresh air. We are all watching for Ma, but nobody wants to say so.

I hang out at the door to Pa's shop awhile, then hop over the timber frame and come in.

"You think Ma had trouble with the truck?" I ask. "You think she got stuck in the mud?"

Pa takes his cap off and rubs his head. "I don't think so, honey. She'll be back soon. Don't worry."

But I am worried. "Were they mean to you at the town offices, Pa, when you were there?"

"They were nice enough, Juice. But they thought

I was some stupid. Because of not reading those letters. I guess they were right, too. I am stupid."

"You're not stupid, Pa. No more than I am. Miss Hamble says some of us are wired up different inside our brains. You and me, we just have a different kind of wiring. You know?"

Pa nods. But he looks like he is carrying a ton of troubles on his back.

"You can learn, Pa. I'm learning. I read those numbers."

Pa nods. "Maybe. Maybe I could. If I had myself a Miss Hamble like you have."

But then he turns away, like that's the last thing he's going to say on this earth. And I go back inside the house.

finding a way

ugar keeps fussing and snorting and fussing and she needs Ma to come back. We all need Ma.

I poke my head into Pa's shop. "Pa, Sugar won't settle to anything. Could you play the fiddle for her?"

Pa comes in and picks up the fiddle and he plays a slow one. Markey dances with the baby. Charleen dances with Turtle. I put my hands out to Lulu, and she takes them. We rock back and forth to Pa's slow music. But then Pa starts a song with a little more kick to it. We sway and sashay all over the kitchen. Sugar stops crying, and her head, tucked against Markey's skinny chest, stops twisting and turning and fussing. Her eyes wide open, she stares at the mess of us Faulstiches, cutting up all over the kitchen floor.

And then the back door opens, and there is Ma, filling the opening, filling it like only Ma can. The sun shines behind her, slipping around the edges of her in the doorway.

The instant Ma enters the kitchen, I swear Sugar starts howling so they could hear her clear to town. Ma sits down and holds Sugar in such a big and generous way. She kisses that baby's eyes and ears and head and settles her in to nurse.

Pa puts his fiddle down, and the bunch of us stand in front of Ma, waiting for her to look up from Sugar.

"Ma, you took too long," Lulu says, finally.

"Too, too, too," says Turtle.

Ma looks up, and her face is pure love. It is such a big love that even though she is holding Sugar, it

feels like she has hold of each and every one of us, too. She is pouring that love into us, and I know, I know even if we don't live in this house anymore, even if we have to leave the little room where all my sisters sleep with me in the two pushed-together beds, even if we have to leave the kitchen with the big green sofa with its humpy sag and its stains and burn spots, even if we have to leave Pa's shop, we'll be all right.

I come up and lean my head on Ma's shoulder. "What'd they say about the house, Ma?"

Ma turns her head so she can kiss me. She plants a solid one square on the top of my head. Feels so good there, like a little helmet of protection from whatever bad news mought be banging down on top of me.

"We've got to save," Ma says. "We've got to save enough to pay back the folks who paid our taxes for us. After that, it'll go easier. They are mighty nice people down there. They said once we pay off those back taxes, even a dollar a week to the town of

Redemption would be enough. We just can't miss any more payments. They say just come and talk about it if we have a problem. Just come and talk."

Pa shakes his head. "But, Glory, we've got that and the thousand-dollar fine, too. How can we pay it all?"

"I talked to Miss Hamble and the principal, Gannon. I explained about Juice missing school on account of her delivering the baby. And they said, 'Mrs. Faulstich, they can't make you pay what you don't have. Don't worry about the fine. Nobody's going to make you pay. We just want you to understand how important it is Juice comes to school.'"

"Will they put Juice in jail?" Lulu asks.

Ma says, "They can't put none of us in jail, honey. I promise. But, Juice, Miss Hamble's waiting that play on you. So you got to go back, and you got to keep going."

I nod.

Ma looks at Pa. "Gannon, you don't worry about

the money. You just keep making your plates and your pitchers and your candlesticks. You keep taking every little job that walks through that door. I'll talk to all the ones we're owing money to. We'll do it. You're a regular business tycoon, Gannon Faulstich, and a fine man, too. You work your metal and play your fiddle, and we'll all make out just fine."

And I can see in my mind that red car turning itself around and heading down the hill, away from our house, and never coming back.

Ma sweeps her eyes over the lot of us. "But y'all listen up," she says.

Sugar pulls off and starts fussing.

Ma shifts the baby over to the other side and settles her in again.

When Ma looks back at us, her face is some cross. "Y'all listening?"

We nod.

"Everybody," Ma says, "I mean everybody in this house is learning to read. Y'all hear me? You understand, Lulu?" Ma sounds stern and she looks stern. She means business.

Lulu puts her hands on her hips. Her mouth opens to argue. Then Ma winks at her.

"And everyone, I mean everyone who is of age, is going to school." Ma smiles at me, and I smile back.

I won't ever catch up with Mrs. Deal's class, but the kids I'm with now, they are nicer to me, anyway. They don't think I'm stupid anymore, just different, thanks to Miss Hamble. And maybe a little thanks to me, too. Ma says when Miss Hamble told them I saved the baby's life and Ma's life, too, the kids in my class said they bet I'd grow up and be some famous doctor someday.

But I know better. I'm glad everything turned out with Ma and Sugar. But if I had to choose between being a doctor or a machinist, I'd rather be in Pa's shop, with the smell and the sound of metal moving just the way I want it to go. I figure it this way: If I can bend metal now, by the time I turn twelve, who knows?

Maybe I can play fiddle.

Maybe I can read a whole book all myself, out

loud, to my baby sister. And she'll look at me the way all of us look at Pa, the way all of us look at Ma.

The thing is, I don't have to be a famous doctor or anything fancy like that to be happy. All I have to be is Juice, just Juice. And that's enough.